A Note to Parents and Caregivers:

Read-it! Readers are for children who are just starting on the amazing road to reading. These beautiful books support both the acquisition of reading skills and the love of books.

 The PURPLE LEVEL presents basic topics and objects using high frequency words and simple language patterns.

 The RED LEVEL presents familiar topics using common words and repeating sentence patterns.

 The BLUE LEVEL presents new ideas using a larger vocabulary and varied sentence structure.

 The YELLOW LEVEL presents more challenging ideas, a broad vocabulary, and wide variety in sentence structure.

 The GREEN LEVEL presents more complex ideas, an extended vocabulary range, and expanded language structures.

 The ORANGE LEVEL presents a wide range of ideas and concepts using challenging vocabulary and complex language structures.

When sharing a book with your child, read in short stretches, pausing often to talk about the pictures. Have your child turn the pages and point to the pictures and familiar words. And be sure to reread favorite stories or parts of stories.

There is no right or wrong way to share books with children. Find time to read with your child, and pass on the legacy of literacy.

Adria F. Klein, Ph.D.
Professor Emeritus
California State University
San Bernardino, California

Editor: Christianne Jones
Designer: Lori Bye
Page Production: Michelle Biedscheid
Art Director: Nathan Gassman
The illustrations in this book were created with watercolor and pencil.

Picture Window Books
151 Good Counsel Drive
P.O. Box 669
Mankato, MN 56002-0669
877-845-8392
www.picturewindowbooks.com

Printed in the United States of America.

 All books published by Picture Window Books
are manufactured with paper containing at least
10 percent post-consumer waste.

Library of Congress Cataloging-in-Publication Data
Worsham, Adria F. (Adria Fay), 1947-
Max celebrates Martin Luther King Jr. Day / by Adria F. Worsham ; illustrated by
Mernie Gallagher-Cole.
p. cm. — (Read-it! readers. The life of Max)
ISBN-13: 978-1-4048-4761-3 (library binding)
1. Martin Luther King, Jr., Day—Juvenile fiction. 2. King, Martin Luther, Jr., 1929-
1968—Juvenile fiction. [1. Martin Luther King, Jr., Day—Fiction. 2. King, Martin
Luther, Jr., 1929-1968—Fiction. 3. Schools—Fiction.] I. Gallagher-Cole, Mernie, ill.
II. Title.
PZ7.W887835Maxx 2008
[E]—dc22   2008006317

Max

Celebrates
Martin Luther King Jr. Day

by Adria F. Worsham
illustrated by Mernie Gallagher-Cole

Special thanks to our reading adviser:

Susan Kesselring, M.A., Literacy Educator
Rosemount–Apple Valley–Eagan (Minnesota) School District

PICTURE WINDOW BOOKS
Minneapolis, Minnesota

Max and his parents are going to celebrate Martin Luther King Jr. Day.

It is always on the third Monday in January.

There will be a special event at school.

At school, the teacher tells Max and his class that Martin Luther King Jr. was an important man.

At the event, there are lots of students and teachers.

There are lots of parents, too.

The principal talks about Martin Luther King Jr.

She says he was a teacher and a preacher.

The principal shows pictures of
Martin Luther King Jr.

She says that Martin Luther King Jr. studied a lot. He went to college and learned many things.

The principal shows more pictures. She talks about all of the important things Martin Luther King Jr. did.

He gave speeches all over the
United States.

Martin Luther King Jr. marched to bring freedom to all people.

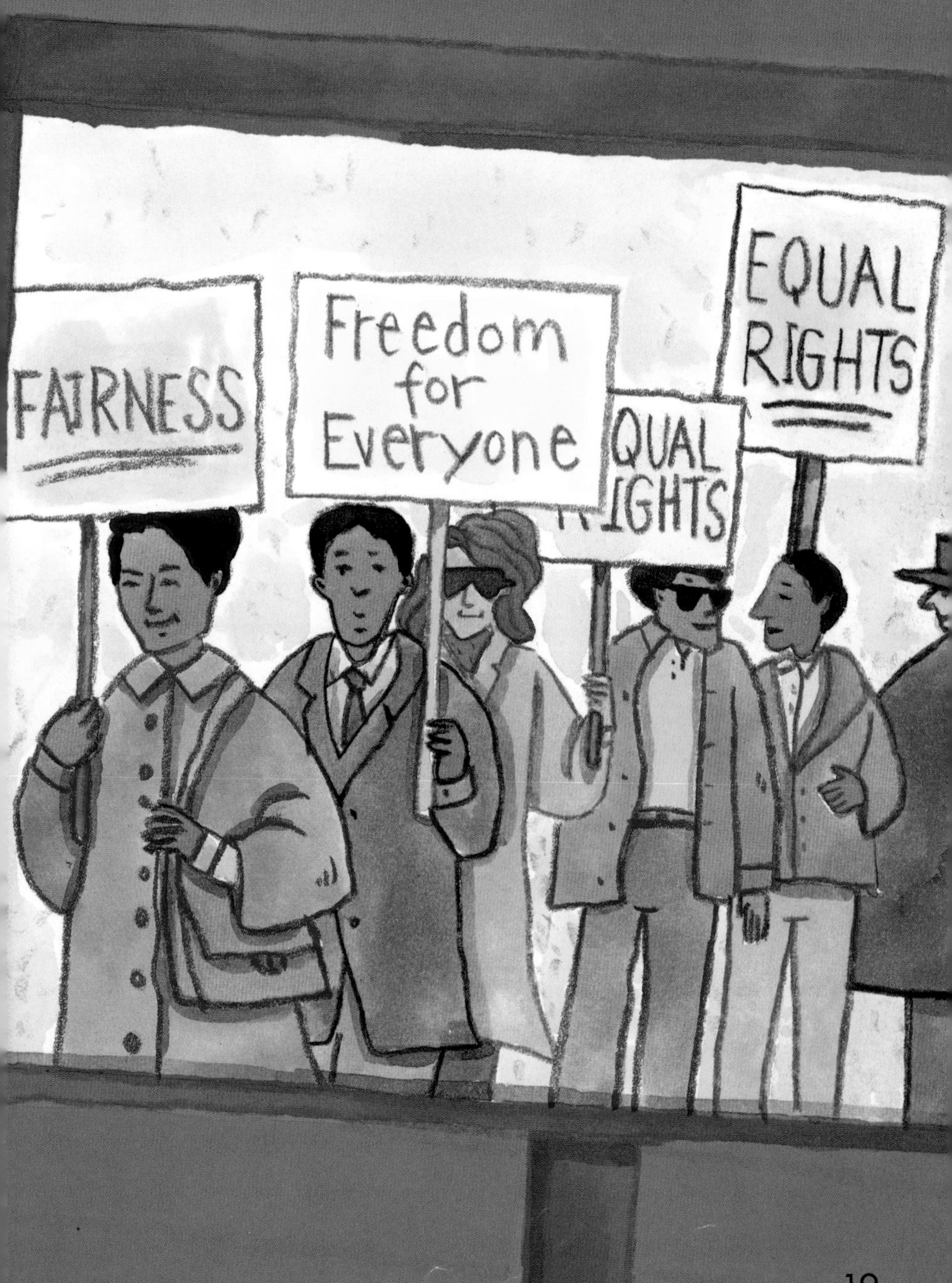
FAIRNESS
Freedom for Everyone
QUAL
IGHTS
EQUAL RIGHTS

Martin Luther King Jr. helped get equal rights for African-Americans.

Max is happy and proud to celebrate
Martin Luther King Jr. Day.

More *Read-it!* Readers

Bright pictures and fun stories help you practice your reading skills.
Look for more books at your level.

Max Goes on the Bus

Max Goes Shopping

Max Goes to School

Max Goes to the Barber

Max Goes to the Dentist

Max Goes to the Doctor

Max Goes to the Library

Max Goes to the Playground

Max and Buddy Go to the Vet

Max and the Adoption Day Party

Max Celebrates Chinese New Year

Max Celebrates Cinco de Mayo

Max Celebrates Groundhog Day

Max Celebrates Ramadan

Max Goes to a Cookout

Max Goes to the Farm

Max Goes to the Grocery Store

Max Learns Sign Language

Max Stays Overnight

Max's Fun Day

On the Web

FactHound offers a safe, fun way to find Web sites related to topics
in this book. All of the sites on FactHound have been researched
by our staff.

1. Visit *www.facthound.com*

2. Type in this special code: 1404847618

3. Click on the FETCH IT button.

Your trusty FactHound will fetch the best sites for you!
A complete list of *Read-it!* Readers is available on our Web site:
www.picturewindowbooks.com

24